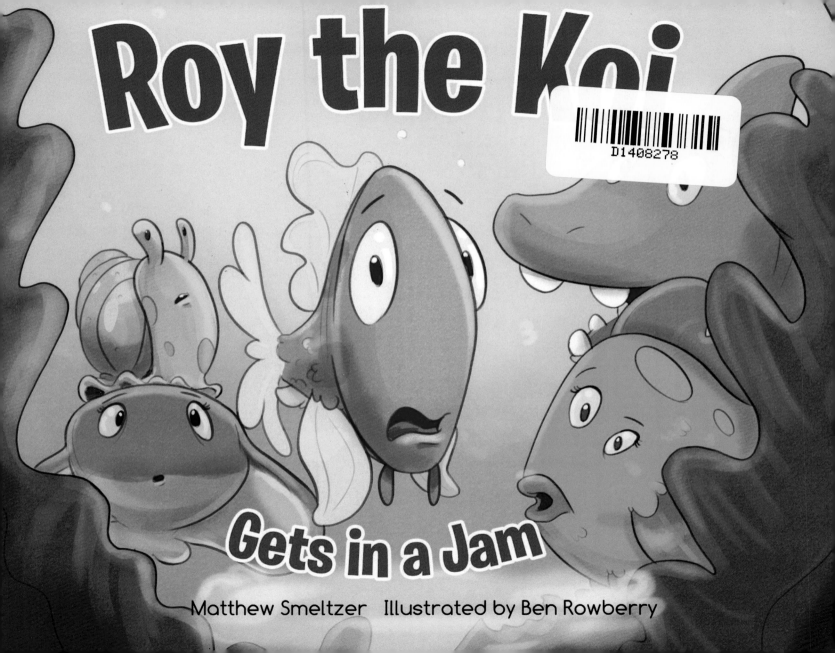

Roy the Koi

Gets in a Jam

Matthew Smeltzer   Illustrated by Ben Rowberry

For my parents, who have always been incredibly supportive and taught me lessons about financial literacy starting at a young age.

Roy the Koi lived in the sea,
in a secret fort where he loved to be.
Roy's secret fort was built of kelp,
and to make it required no one's help.

Deep in his fort, Roy saved some clams,
to only use if he got in a jam.

Roy the Koi had lots of good friends,
who were all obsessed with the latest trends.

He went to visit Freya the Flounder.
Roy always had fun when he was around her.

Freya the Flounder had so many toys,
some were small and others tall.
Toys that flew and toys that grew.
Toys that sang and toys that went BANG!

Roy loved Freya's newest toy.
Playing with it brought him much joy!
Freya suggested, "Buy your own at the store.
Then we can play with them down at the shore!"

"As much as I would like to," said Roy, "I cannot spend my clams. You see, I need to save them, in case I'm ever in a jam."

After playing with Freya, Roy headed to the park.
There he saw his friend, whose name was Sally the Shark.

Sally the Shark loved clothes and wore the latest fashions.
Clothing and jewelry were her greatest passions.

Sally had blouses, skirts, boas, and lockets.

She had many types of clothes,
most of them had several bows.

Don't forget, shirts and pants
with fancy pockets!

Roy loved Sally's yellow polka-dot boots
and wished for a pair to go with his suit!
Sally urged, "Spend your clams to buy some new clothes.
Then we could put on our own fashion shows!"

"As much as I would like to," said Roy, "I cannot spend my clams. You see, I need to save them, in case I'm ever in a jam."

After talking to Sally, Roy headed to the bay,
where he met another friend, whose name was Remy the Ray!
Remy loved candy: chocolates, caramels, mints, and gummies.
All of them he found very yummy!

"Roy, please sit down and take a rest.
Try some of these chocolates, they are the best!"

Roy tried the chocolates and thought they were great!
Remy pointed, "Buy more at the store, beyond the green gate."

"As much as I would like to," said Roy, "I cannot spend my clams. You see, I need to save them, in case I'm ever in a jam."

Then Roy swam back to his fort of kelp.
Once he arrived, Roy saw he needed help!

While Roy was out enjoying the day,
a starfish had nibbled most of his fort away!

Roy called his friend, named Sammy the Snail.
He said, "Come to my shop to see what's for sale."

At the repair shop, searching aisles near and far,
Sammy then shouted, "Over here, by the jar!

This is a kelp kit, which will cost you ten clams.
Surely it will help you get out of your jam!"

Roy bought the kit and hurried back to his fort,
to fix the kelp, which had been nibbled quite short.

After fixing his fort, Roy thought back on his day.
"Wow, I'm glad I did not spend my clams in any other way!

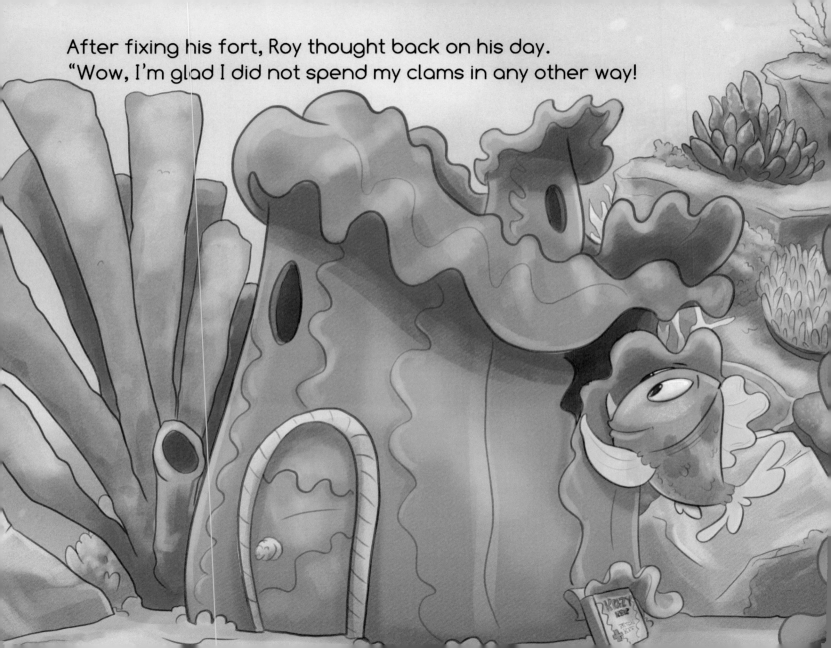

If I had bought toys, clothes, or even candy,
I could not buy the kit, which came in very handy."

"So, you see, I will STILL save my clams, to use whenever I get in a jam."

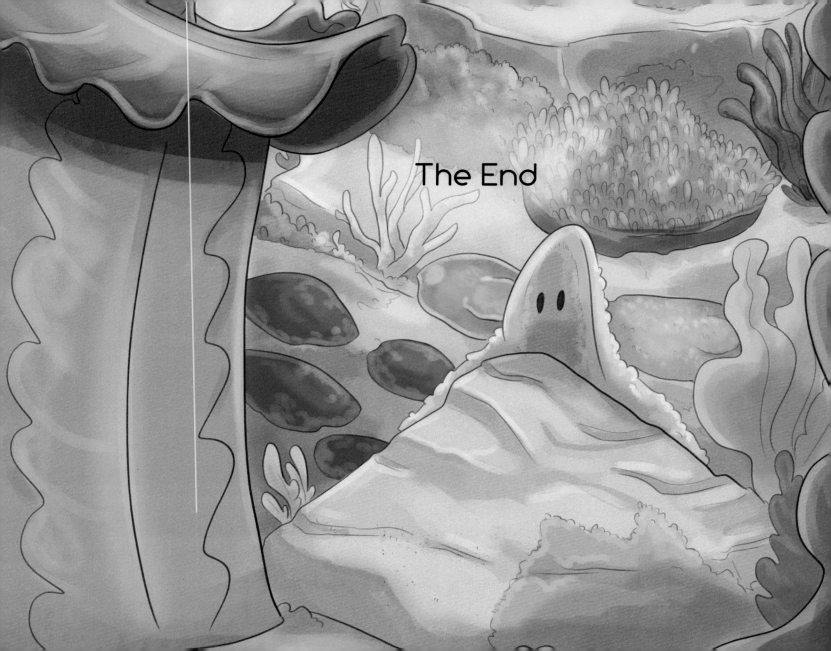

The End